Beyond th...

B...18

Mith Ickle
Rocky Nook
Dragon's Valley
Bellua

Dear Mith Ickle,

Well, I've never written to a dragon before, but it looks like I haven't got any choice.

Things are just _so_ bad over here at the Frozen Merlakes. You'll never believe it, but one of our younger mermaids has had all her colours stolen. Honestly, I've never seen a mermaid's tail look _so_ ugly! Now she can't swim, or move around, or really do _anything_. Of course, the rest of us mermaids have to look after her all the time, which is pretty boring, I can tell you.

Nothing we've tried has made her better so we need to ask the Guardian for help. I've heard you're friends with her so can you ask her to come to us? Like _now_? We all think that evil Imp King has got something to do with it. You have to help us fix this before anything else happens around here – or in the rest of Bellua!

And do hurry, won't you?

Ariana
(Golden-haired mermaid with beautiful coloured tail)

Read all the adventures of

THE DRAGON'S SONG

THE UNICORN'S HORN

THE FAIRY'S WING

THE MERMAID'S TAIL

The Mermaid's Tail

CLAIRE TAYLOR-SMITH

Illustrated by Lorena Alvarez

PUFFIN

PUFFIN BOOKS

Published by the Penguin Group
Penguin Books Ltd, 80 Strand, London WC2R ORL, England
Penguin Group (USA) Inc., 375 Hudson Street, New York, New York 10014, USA
Penguin Group (Canada), 90 Eglinton Avenue East, Suite 700, Toronto, Ontario, Canada M4P 2Y3
(a division of Pearson Penguin Canada Inc.)
Penguin Ireland, 25 St Stephen's Green, Dublin 2, Ireland (a division of Penguin Books Ltd)
Penguin Group (Australia), 707 Collins Street, Melbourne, Victoria 3008, Australia
(a division of Pearson Australia Group Pty Ltd)
Penguin Books India Pvt Ltd, 11 Community Centre, Panchsheel Park, New Delhi – 110 017, India
Penguin Group (NZ), 67 Apollo Drive, Rosedale, Auckland 0632, New Zealand
(a division of Pearson New Zealand Ltd)
Penguin Books (South Africa) (Pty) Ltd, Block D, Rosebank Office Park,
181 Jan Smuts Avenue, Parktown North, Gauteng 2193, South Africa

Penguin Books Ltd, Registered Offices: 80 Strand, London WC2R ORL, England

puffinbooks.com

First published 2014
001

Text and illustrations copyright © Penguin Books Ltd, 2014
Story concept originated by Mums Creative Content Ltd
Illustrations by Lorena Alvarez
With thanks to Claire Baker
Set in 14.5/24pt Bembo Book MT Std
Typeset by Jouve (UK), Milton Keynes
Printed in Great Britain by Clays Ltd, St Ives plc
British Library Cataloguing in Publication Data
A CIP catalogue record for this book is available from the British Library

ISBN: 978-0-141-34466-9

www.greenpenguin.co.uk

Penguin Books is committed to a sustainable
future for our business, our readers and our planet.
This book is made from Forest Stewardship
Council™ certified paper.

With love to Louie, Hope and Seth,

who have taken me on many

magical adventures of their own x

Winter
Mountains

Cave

Valley
of the
Guardians

Pixie
Park

Elf Avenue

Dragons
Valley

Silvery Stream

Unicorn
Meadows

Enchanted
Orchard

Rumbling
Volcano

Troll
Bridge

Fairy Forest

Rainbow
Waterfall

Ancient
Desert

Hidden
Lake

Frozen
Merlakes

Contents

The Call to Bellua

Standing on the village green with her best friend Chloe, Hattie Bright was admiring a large cream building with wide blue doors and a red roof.

'I can't believe it's finally ready,' said Chloe, looking at the recently finished village hall.

'And our drama group's going to be the first to show off the new stage!' said Hattie excitedly.

A few children from her class had prepared

a short play, which they were going to perform as soon as the mayor cut the ribbon and declared the hall officially open. 'Aren't we on in less than half an hour?' she added, glancing at her watch nervously.

'Yep,' agreed Chloe. 'We'd better hurry up and get ready!'

Backstage several of Hattie's classmates were already getting into their costumes, while crowded round the only mirror were Victoria Frost and her friends Jodie and Louisa. A large assortment of make-up was spread out in front of them.

'A second eyeshadow colour or not?' asked

Victoria, sweeping a flash of shimmering green across an eyelid.

'I think you look lovely already,' simpered Jodie, before Louisa quickly added: 'Whatever you do will look perfect, Victoria.'

Victoria was just about to apply some silver to the green when Hattie's reflection appeared in the mirror behind her own.

'I hope you're not going to ask to use the mirror, Hattie,' sneered Victoria, before Hattie even had a chance to open her mouth. 'Only, I've got to do Jodie and Louisa after me and we don't have much time left.'

'It's OK, I'll get changed first,' Hattie said cheerfully, deciding there was no time for an argument either. 'I don't think my character needs much make-up anyway.'

Soon Hattie and Chloe were in their costumes, a light brushing of powder applied to both their faces.

'I'm going to leave my hair down,' said Chloe. 'How about you, Hattie?'

'Well, I was going to have bunches, but I'm not sure I can do them myself, especially without a mirror,' replied Hattie.

'I can help you in a minute,' said Chloe, 'but I just need to sort out these trousers first. They keep falling down!'

As Chloe rushed off to rummage through the costume chest for a belt, Hattie was surprised to hear Victoria behind her.

'Bunches, did you say, Hattie? I could help you do those. Jodie and Louisa *always* say I'm brilliant

at hairstyles and you've got such, um . . . *unusual* hair, it would be a real treat to style it for you.'

'It's OK. Chloe said she'd –' began Hattie, but Victoria already had one half of Hattie's long dark hair grasped in her hand.

'Oh, seeing as I've already started, I may as well finish,' said Victoria. 'Now, do you want that white streak in one bunch or split between two?'

With her bunches in place, Hattie was looking around for Chloe when a familiar voice rang out. 'Knock, knock! Hello! Anyone called Hattie here? Hattie B?'

'Uncle B!' Half-embarrassed and half-amused at his sudden appearance backstage, Hattie ran over to greet her uncle. 'I didn't know you'd be here!'

'What, miss seeing my niece in her starring role?' said Uncle B. 'I remember once when I played Dick Whittington in a school play – I took my own tabby cat in and she flew right up the stage curtains. Took three days and two tins of cat food to lure her down again. Last big role my drama teacher gave me, unfortunately . . .'

'Mine's not exactly a starring role,' said Hattie. 'It's only a few lines with Chloe towards the middle, but we've practised them loads.'

'Ah yes, practice, that's the key,' said Uncle B. 'And of course speaking loudly, clearly and always to the person right at the back of the hall – that's so that everyone can hear you, you know. You'll never go wrong with good speaking skills, Hattie. Who knows when they might come in handy?'

'Thanks, Uncle B, I'll remember that,' said Hattie. 'I just hope I don't forget my words.'

'Ah well, if things don't go to plan, you'll have to think on your feet and improvise. I know you'll be good at that, Hattie. We Brights have to be – well, some of us more than others. Never know where we might find ourselves, eh?' he said with a wink. 'Anyway, good luck, Hattie. Break a leg – isn't that what they say? Not that I'd want you to break one really, of course. That wouldn't help with –' He stopped mid-sentence and his eyes darted quickly from side to side. 'Oh, never mind! Good luck!'

'Wouldn't help with what?' asked Hattie, but Uncle B had already disappeared with a loud 'Cheerio!'.

Wouldn't help with what? Hattie wondered again to herself. She suspected her uncle knew more about the magical Kingdom of Bellua than he was letting on. Glancing at the charm bracelet dangling from her wrist,

Hattie saw she'd guessed right. The star, dragon, unicorn and fairy charms attached to it were already taking on their tell-tale glow. Somewhere in Bellua a creature needed her help.

There's no time to lose, thought Hattie. *I'll have to think of an excuse to sneak out quickly!*

Before she could think of a plan, though, she was swept along by the other children as they headed towards the stage.

'I'd like to welcome you all to our lovely new village hall!' boomed the mayor. Everyone backstage could hear him clearly. 'Now please

take your seats for a drama presentation by some of our talented children.'

Hattie looked at the bracelet again and saw that the charms were glowing brighter and

brighter. She quickly tucked it up her sleeve so that no one would spot it. She could hear the audience scraping their chairs as they sat down, and a hush descended as they waited for the play to start.

'*Phew!* Found a belt just in time,' whispered Chloe, suddenly appearing at Hattie's side. 'What's up with your wrist? I saw you looking at it about a million times.'

'Only a million?' joked Hattie, trying to cover her sleeve with her other hand to make completely sure the bracelet couldn't be seen. She was under an oath of secrecy and couldn't risk her best friend getting too curious. She laughed off Chloe's question with a change of subject. 'What do you think of my hair anyway? You'll never believe who did it for me – Victoria! I wasn't sure I should let her, but she was actually quite nice to me for once.'

'It looks a bit . . .' began Chloe, but then the opening music filled the entire hall and drowned her out completely.

As the music got louder, Hattie knew it was now or never. Remembering that no time passed in the real world when she was called to Bellua, she made her mind up.

'I've got to get something, a prop – for my character,' she whispered to Chloe, grateful that the still-thumping music made it difficult for her to be heard properly. She began to step away, mouthing reassuring words at her confused friend as she went. 'Don't worry. I'll be back in ten minutes flat. I won't miss our big entrance, I promise!'

As she dashed away, Hattie tried not to think about the concerned look on her friend's face. Hattie would have to get used to making excuses if she was going to be a successful Guardian. On her previous visit, King Ivar of the Imps had said he would stop at nothing to seize magic from the poor, defenceless creatures of Bellua, so she had to protect them. She hoped she would get there quickly enough. They would be counting on her!

An image of Ivar's mean, scowling face flashed before her. He'd stolen the power of flight from a fairy the last time she'd been there. Who knew what he would take next?

Full of resolve, Hattie ran home as fast as she could . . .

Bright Lights

Once inside her empty house, Hattie dashed up the stairs and into her bedroom. She ducked under her bed and, as quickly as she could, she pulled out a battered old vet's bag – her gateway to the magical Kingdom of Bellua.

As soon as she placed the glowing star charm on her bracelet over the bag's lock, the bag sprang open with a familiar click, releasing a small puff of fairy dust. Hattie smiled as she remembered how grateful her last patient, the little fairy Titch, had been. Then she watched in wonder as the bag's dull leather turned to sparkly silver and the letters *H* and *B* appeared.

Knowing exactly what to do, she poked her head into the open bag and, feeling a surge of nervous excitement, found herself tumbling down, down and down . . .

Hattie gave a little *whoop* of excitement when she arrived back in the Guardian's cave. She was really pleased that she had landed squarely on her feet!

Mith Ickle, who was perched on the vet's table, congratulated Hattie with three short puffs of smoke.

'Mith! It's *so* nice to see you again!' called Hattie, making her way towards the little pink dragon.

Looking down, Hattie was surprised to see that she was in her normal clothes, and not the costume that she had been wearing back in the real world. She supposed it made sense, as Bellua was a *magical* world after all, and she couldn't really carry out her Guardian's duties in fancy dress!

As her eyes adjusted to being inside the cave, Hattie realized it was much darker than usual.

The crystals on the walls were reflecting the light from a single candle on the table next to Mith Ickle, giving the cave a dull glow.

'Why are you sitting in the dark, Mith?' asked Hattie. 'Let me uncover the window.'

'NO!' cried Mith Ickle, before Hattie had taken more than a step towards the small window in one wall of the cave. 'I put that cloth over it to protect you. I'm afraid something strange is going on.'

Hattie felt a lurch of fear in her stomach. 'What do you mean by "strange", Mith?' she asked.

'I knew you'd arrive soon so I came here to wait,' continued her friend, 'but on the way flashes of light filled the sky. They were so bright I thought they might hurt your eyes, and I covered the window just in case.'

'Could it be something to do with –'

Mith Ickle sighed. 'King Ivar? Yes, I think it probably could. He's more determined than ever to make himself the ruler of Bellua. All the creatures are saying he's getting better and better at using his stolen powers – only yesterday he froze the pixies half to death by sending a snowstorm into Pixie Park!'

'Oh, poor little things! Are they OK now?' asked Hattie.

'Yes, they all huddled together inside a hollow tree until the storm passed. No one was hurt, but they heard Ivar laughing, which scared them more than the storm itself!'

'He's getting more confident,' Hattie mumbled to herself. 'But who needs my help this time, Mith? Is my patient here already?' she asked, glancing around the cave. (She was never quite sure what size the creature that needed her help would be.)

'No, she's not here. It's a mermaid called Marina,' replied the dragon. 'I'm not sure how he's done it, but Ivar has stolen the magic colour from her tail. It's causing her all kinds of problems – she can't use her tail to see in the dark, or to camouflage herself if she needs to hide. I've heard she can't even slide into the merlake for a swim. Without her magic, she's too sick to go anywhere at all.'

Mith Ickle went on to explain that a mermaid couldn't stay on land forever – she'd start to dry out and get weaker.

'We'll have to go to her straight away, Mith, and we'll do whatever it takes to help her regain her lost colours. But first I need to find out how to treat her.'

Hattie knew exactly where to look . . .

Hattie's confidence grew when she felt the soft red leather of the *Healing Magickal Beastes & Creatures* book under her fingertips.

'I remember seeing a section on mermaids last time I was here,' said Hattie as she began to leaf through the pages, squinting in the dim light. 'Now, where was it?'

'This might help,' said Mith Ickle, flying above Hattie's head and perching on a shelf behind her. 'A dragon lamp!' And the little dragon shot out a small, flickering flame that provided enough light to allow Hattie to find what she was looking for.

'*Mermaid malaise*,' Hattie read aloud. 'I think that means "mermaid illnesses", Mith. It says here that *a mermaid relieved of colour will also be relieved of strengthe and well-being in equal measure. No longer may she employe her colours to escape danger; no longer may she fire her greatest weapon.'*

Hattie was puzzled. What kind of weapon would a mermaid have? There was only one

Mermaids

fig. 6a

c. Tail.

fig 7

• A Mermaid relieved of colour will also be

Scales

way to find out – they would have to make their way to the Frozen Merlakes as quickly as they could!

'This must be the right bit, Mith,' said Hattie eagerly, running her finger down the page, where tiny neat writing was filling the paper at great speed. 'Yes, here we are: *How to restore a mermaid's vanished colours*. Looks like this is what we have to find.'

At a magickal waterfall, ruled by might,
Flow many healing colours bright.
Speak well to win this syrupy cure,
Which many have foregone before.

'The magical waterfall with the "colours bright" must be the Rainbow Waterfall,' said Hattie.

'Yes,' said Mith. 'And there's a rainbow syrup too, but it's very hard to get it.'

For a moment, Hattie felt her enthusiasm slide away. Would she be able to get the rainbow syrup if others had already failed? And what did the rhyme mean about speaking well? Uncle B's words at the village hall came back to her: *You'll never go wrong with good speaking skills, Hattie. Who knows when they might come in handy?* Perhaps Uncle B had known a new challenge was coming her way after all.

'Come on, Mith,' she said, grabbing the map, which as usual had fluttered on to the table. 'I reckon we need to head to the Rainbow Waterfall to get our cure. We'll visit Marina in the Frozen Merlakes first and make sure she's comfortable. Maybe the mermaids will be able to tell us what to expect when we get there. I just hope that they're a little more friendly than the last mermaids we met!'

'Me too,' agreed Mith Ickle, extinguishing her flickering flame and hopping down from the shelf. 'Those mermaids were grumpier than a damp dragon in December! Now, let's make sure the coast's clear before we step outside.'

Hattie very slowly pulled back the sheet that covered the little window, while Mith Ickle told her to be careful because the bright flashing lights might suddenly appear. With relief, the two friends saw that all seemed to be back to normal in the Kingdom of Bellua.

'It looks like Ivar's gone to cause trouble somewhere else for now,' said the little dragon as they left the cave, although her eyes still darted anxiously from side to side.

'Thanks for looking out for me,' said Hattie. 'I don't expect that's the last we'll see of Ivar today, though, do you?'

As Mith Ickle nodded in agreement, Hattie strode towards her next adventure.

Miserable Mermaids

As the two friends hurried towards the Frozen Merlakes, the beauty of Bellua made Hattie catch her breath in wonder.

Mith Ickle pointed towards a copper-coloured streak in the air around them and said it was a group of fire sprites. Hattie watched wide-eyed as the tiny creatures waved to her enthusiastically before heading towards a most unusual bush. It was laden with bright orange and yellow flowers that seemed to be gently puffing out smoke instead of pollen!

In the distance Hattie spotted a huge rainbow that spanned the sparkling sky, each band of colour ending in its own light shower of raindrops. Even the grass beneath Hattie's feet was like no other grass. It was velvet soft and such an even green it looked like a carpet of emeralds.

When the friends left the lush grass to join the path to Pixie Park, something caught Mith Ickle's eye.

'What's that pile of clothes doing there, Hattie?' she asked, indicating a little top and trousers that were bundled together under a bush. 'Don't you think they look a bit like Immie's?'

'Anyone could have left them there,' said Hattie, 'although I can't imagine why they would.'

Mith Ickle looked thoughtful. 'Those imps are always up to mischief,' she said with a snort. 'It's bound to be one of their silly games.'

Speeding up, Hattie hurried past the Enchanted Orchard and soon found herself, teeth chattering, at the Frozen Merlakes.

The mermaids were gathered in groups round the merlakes, but none of them greeted Hattie and Mith Ickle. A couple gave them a brief glance, but most carried on brushing their long hair or whispering to each other in voices too low for Hattie to hear. Although their rudeness came as no surprise, Hattie couldn't help being

just as amazed at their flawless beauty as she had been before.

Wondering where her patient might be, Hattie began to walk along the edge of the first lake, wrapping her arms round her shivering body. A gentle ripple in the water moved towards them and a mermaid with bright blue eyes and rose-blushed cheeks appeared. To Hattie's surprise, she swam straight over and spoke to her directly.

'You must be the Guardian. If you're looking for Marina, she's over there by that snowberry bush.' The mermaid pointed a little further round the lake, before adding, 'You will be able to help her, won't you?'

'I hope so,' replied Hattie. 'Thanks for telling me where to find her.' But the mermaid had already swum away.

Hattie soon found Marina, a young mermaid who was lying on an ice-covered rock, accompanied by two older mermaids. Her pale grey-white tail was in sharp contrast to the tails of the other mermaids, which shone in an incredible range of colours, their blues, greens, pinks and purples all shimmering brightly in the icy air. Marina looked tired – her long hair was a dull mousey-brown and in desperate need of a brush.

'Hello, you must be Marina,' said Hattie, crouching down beside the stricken mermaid, grateful for the warmth of Mith Ickle's body round her shoulders. 'I'm Hattie. I've come to help you.'

Marina groaned. 'Thank you,' she said. 'I

can't move my tail or control my colour, which means I can't even swim, let alone camouflage myself underwater. If I don't get back into the water soon, my tail will dry out completely.'

Hattie nodded gently with concern, trying to ignore the sniffs and tuts of the other mermaids who had swum over from around the lake. Were they annoyed that she'd come to help? Hattie wasn't sure, but, whether she was welcome or not, she knew she couldn't leave Marina in this state. She had made an oath to treat *every* creature in Bellua – she was not going to let Ivar have his evil way!

'Don't worry, Marina. I'm here to help you,' said Hattie in her friendliest voice. 'Do you know how you ended up losing your colours in the first place?'

'It was that awful Imp King!' spat one of the other mermaids. 'I saw him from the other side of the lake – he hid behind this rock and looked like he was whispering something to Marina. She drifted off to sleep straight away!'

'I do remember hearing a song . . .' said Marina weakly.

'That was *my* song he was singing!' squawked Mith Ickle, puffing up with annoyance. 'He stole it from me a while ago. We dragons use it to send people to sleep, but only when we *really* have to. It's against the Dragon Code to misuse it!'

'What happened next?' Hattie asked Marina.

'I don't know,' said Marina feebly. 'I was fast asleep and, when I woke up again, my tail looked like *this*.' She pointed miserably at her outstretched tail, where the dull scales were lying flat and lifeless. 'It's useless and ugly and I feel so weak.'

'It looks like your friends have been looking after you at least,' said Hattie, trying to stay positive.

The mermaids let out a chorus of snorts.

'Only because we have to,' said one mermaid with long auburn ringlets.

'Can't you just fix her tail?' asked another.

'Then we won't have to do this boring sitting around any more,' sneered a third.

That's not very nice! thought Hattie. *These mermaids make Victoria Frost look kind!*

Marina didn't seem too upset by the mermaids' nasty comments, though.

'Do you know how to mend it?' she asked hopefully. 'I know that's what Guardians are supposed to do. But you're new, aren't you?' she added, barely hiding her concern that Hattie wouldn't be up to the job.

'Well, I do have something to try,' said Hattie a little defensively, 'but it might not be easy to get hold of. There's a special syrup that should bring your colours back. It's at the

44

Rainbow Waterfall. I'll come back with it as soon as I can.'

The gasp that followed this statement was so loud it made Hattie jump. She looked around to see several mermaids staring at her, their mouths wide open in horror.

'Well, I don't like Marina's chances then!' said the auburn-haired mermaid. 'The High Mermaid will *never* let you have any of her precious rainbow syrup. She couldn't care less if we lake mermaids live or die. You might as well give up hope now, Marina!'

'High Mermaid?' asked Hattie. 'Who's she?'

'Oh, for goodness' sake!' huffed the third mermaid. 'Don't you know? I thought *everyone*

had heard of the head of the Mermaid Council. She's the most bad-tempered mermaid in Bellua. We lowly mermaids can't travel across land, obviously, so we've never been to the Council. Not that she'd let us in, anyway. I've heard she'll take offence at anything – throwing visitors out if they cough, sneeze or even pause at the wrong moment when talking to her. Oh, it's completely hopeless!'

'Never give up hope,' said Hattie, wondering whether she could take her own advice as confidently as she gave it. 'I'm sure I can win over this High Mermaid. I've just got to cross the Ancient Desert, then I'll be back before you know it.'

'The Ancient Desert?' cried the auburn-haired mermaid. 'Oh, I wouldn't go that way if I were you. You're better off heading back towards the Enchanted Orchard, then following the Silvery Stream round the edge of the desert.'

'Really?' asked Hattie, wondering if she should trust this advice. 'Won't that take me twice as long?'

'Well, it won't take as long as getting lost. *Everyone* loses their way in the Ancient Desert and I don't see why a Guardian would be any different.'

'OK,' agreed Hattie, ignoring the mermaid's jibe. 'Come on, Mith. It sounds like we have a long journey ahead of us!'

'Please hurry, Hattie!' moaned Marina.

With thoughts of the scary High Mermaid swirling around in her head, Hattie left the poorly mermaid. She led Mith Ickle away from the Frozen Merlakes and, following the map, headed towards the fruit-laden trees of the Enchanted Orchard.

Tricks and Tips

'I'm sure those mermaids do care about each other really, Mith. They just wouldn't dream of showing it!' laughed Hattie as she hurried past the orchard and towards the Silvery Stream. 'I hope it doesn't take us too long to get the rainbow syrup. That poor mermaid is going to feel worse and worse until she drinks some.'

'I know,' agreed Mith Ickle, looking concerned. 'But I'm worried about the stolen colours as well. The magic could be put to all sorts of dangerous uses in the wrong hands.'

'Like Ivar's, you mean?'

'Exactly. Not only can a mermaid change her tail colours when she's in and out of the water, as Marina said, but she can also use them to camouflage herself and hide from enemies –'

'Which means Ivar will be able to camouflage himself now,' finished Hattie.

Mith Ickle nodded. 'I just remembered there's something else he could do as well,' said the little dragon. 'When a mermaid senses *real* danger, she can combine all her colours to make the brightest white, which she shoots out in a beam of light. It can be almost blinding.'

'Which would explain the flashes you saw on your way to the cave,' said Hattie.

Mith Ickle nodded again. 'So Ivar's putting his new power to the test already.'

Even at a half-run, Hattie could see it would take them a long time to reach the Rainbow Waterfall. Every so often she peeked at the map that she'd tucked into her trouser pocket to check they were going the right way. But, although she was sure they were, the path was long and windy, and they never seemed to be that far along it.

When Hattie spotted a multicoloured shimmer in the sky ahead, she thought they might finally be near their destination.

'Look, Mith, can you see the colours over there?' she cried. 'That must be the Rainbow Waterfall. We're almost there!'

Keeping her gaze on the shifting hues filling the sky, she quickened her pace.

'Do you think the High Mermaid's as awful as they say she is?' asked Hattie.

'Well, I've never met her myself, but I have heard she can be quite fearsome,' replied Mith Ickle, almost as out of breath as her friend. 'One of my cousins flew over the Rainbow Waterfall by mistake once, and the High Mermaid made her whole Mermaid Guard splash him so hard that they nearly extinguished his flame forever!'

'A Mermaid Guard!' exclaimed Hattie. 'She must be *really* important!'

Suddenly a small voice interrupted their conversation. 'Oh yes! You wouldn't want to upset the High Mermaid. She really can be quite terrifying if she takes a dislike to you.'

A curious-looking pixie had stepped out in front of them.

'Hattie . . . er, or is it, um, Hetty? I mean, we've never met before, have we?' said the pixie. 'Anyway, I heard there was a new Guardian who's a girl and I sort of guessed it must be you.'

Hattie nodded, squinting at the pixie to see whether she recognized her.

'I couldn't help overhearing you talking about going to see the High Mermaid,' the pixie continued. 'I've had the misfortune of meeting

her myself so I can offer you some advice. I'm, er . . . Petunia, by the way. Lovely to meet you.'

'And you,' replied Hattie, crouching down so that she could hear Petunia's tiny voice more easily. 'You're right. I *am* Hattie and I *am* off to see the High Mermaid. When did you meet her?'

'It was, um, a while ago. A week maybe. No, longer than that. A month. Two months maybe. Yes, two or three months ago.'

What a strange creature, Hattie thought.

'I went to ask her something. A question. Nothing important,' said Petunia.

There was something familiar about this pixie, but Hattie couldn't figure out what it was. 'OK,' she said. 'So did she help you?'

'Well, yes, but only after I asked her my question in *exactly* the right way.'

'That makes sense after what the mermaids told us,' said Hattie to Mith Ickle, before turning back to Petunia. 'We heard she can be tricky. So what do you mean by "exactly the right way"?'

'Well, I can give you three pieces of advice for winning her over,' said Petunia, looking pleased with herself.

Hattie smiled. 'That would really help. Thanks, Petunia.'

'The first thing to remember,' she began, 'is that the High Mermaid *hates* loud voices. If I were you, I'd talk to her almost in a whisper.

She's got really good hearing so shouting hurts her ears and makes her very cross.'

'One: don't shout,' Hattie confirmed to herself.

'The second thing is to never repeat *anything*,' Petunia went on, 'even if she asks you to. It's her little trick, you see. Because, if you say something twice, the High Mermaid will accuse you of making her look stupid, as if she hadn't understood what you said in the first place.'

'Two: never repeat anything,' muttered Hattie, although she wondered what she *would* do if the High Mermaid said, '*Pardon?*' – should she assume it was a trick?

There was no time to ask, as Petunia was already on to her third piece of advice. 'Lastly, never answer her questions with a simple *yes* or *no*. Try to turn your answers into riddles, then she'll think you're really clever. Or that she's really clever. Or that you're very clever for making her look very clever. Or something like that. The High Mermaid loves the chance to show off how smart she is, you know!'

'Three: make up riddles,' mumbled Hattie, trying to make sense of Petunia's gabbling.

Realizing that time was tight, she thanked the pixie for her advice, said a quick goodbye and beckoned Mith Ickle to follow her.

'Bye, Hattie!' called Petunia with a giggle

as she skipped off. 'And good luck — you'll need it!'

'What a strange pixie!' said Mith Ickle as she and Hattie continued to make their way towards the colours that filled the sky. 'I'm pretty sure I saw a strand of blue in her hair. You don't think it could be –'

But the little dragon's question remained unfinished as Hattie stopped abruptly.

They'd finally reached a huge gate that rose high above them. It was made of blue and green glass, with delicate trails of fine silver and gold running through it. Perched either side on shimmering gold columns were two mermaids, one dark-haired and one blonde.

Both had tails swirled with rainbow shades, but their beautiful faces were spoilt by their identical scowls.

'We're here, Mith,' said Hattie. 'Are you ready to meet the High Mermaid?'

Before Mith Ickle could answer, the dark-haired mermaid screeched in a shrill voice: 'Surely the question is whether Her Grace the High Mermaid is ready to meet *you*?'

Hattie Speaks Out

'So you wish to enter the Mermaid Council, do you?' asked the dark-haired mermaid. 'Tell me why you've come.'

Keeping her voice calm and clear, Hattie replied, 'I'm Hattie, Guardian of the creatures of the magical Kingdom of Bellua. A mermaid called Marina has had her colours stolen. I need to ask the High Mermaid if she can spare me some rainbow syrup. It's the only cure.'

The expression on the mermaid's face gave nothing away. Hattie couldn't be sure that her explanation had been believed, but then the ornate gate swung open and the memaid said, 'Go to the next rock, Guardian.'

Through the gate, Hattie saw a line of rocks that were evenly spaced along a wide marble path beside a lake. Mermaids were sitting on every boulder, each one dipping her tail into the clear blue lake behind her. They watched Hattie closely as she stepped on to the path, with Mick Ickle flapping alongside her.

At the end of the path, sitting on a gold

throne encrusted with crystals and lined with
brilliant green seaweed, was the High Mermaid.
Compared to the other mermaids, her hair was
longer, curlier and shinier, and her tail more
glossy and colourful. Her folded arms ended in

slim pale hands, and her long, pointed nails were the brightest emerald green. On her head sat a crown made from the most beautiful coral Hattie had ever seen – and just below it was a pale face with a small pinched mouth and two piercingly blue eyes that were staring right at her . . .

'The High Mermaid,' Hattie gasped, 'and she looks absolutely *terrifying*, Mith!'

'Be brave, Hattie,' replied the little dragon. 'Remember, you haven't failed a task yet.'

Hattie felt a small rush of pride at Mith Ickle's statement and, taking a deep breath, she walked purposefully towards the High Mermaid.

'Stop there!' called the mermaid on the rock

nearest to Hattie. 'Don't take another step until you are given permission!'

Shocked at the fierceness of the mermaid's order, Hattie halted immediately and wasn't surprised to feel Mith Ickle curl comfortingly round her shoulders.

'Do nothing and say nothing in the presence of Her Grace the High Mermaid until you are asked to do so. Now move to the next rock.'

Hattie obeyed silently.

The mermaid at the next rock wasn't any friendlier. She insisted that Hattie stood straighter and brushed her hair off her face in the High Mermaid's presence. Hattie's nerves were building with each instruction she was given as she moved from one stern mermaid to the next.

Her fears were only interrupted by a loud shriek that broke into her thoughts. 'I said move on to the next rock. NOW!'

Hattie didn't waste any time apologizing to the furious mermaid for her hesitation, and she quickly hurried on.

The next mermaid didn't make any demands. Instead she raised an elegant arm and pointed in the direction of the High Mermaid's beautiful golden throne.

'You may address Her Grace now,' she told Hattie. 'Take your position on the silver Speaker's Rock and remember what you have been told – there will be consequences if you don't. Go!'

With the instructions given by the various mermaids mingling in her head along with Petunia's advice, Hattie approached the rock of glittering silver crystals and stepped purposefully on to it.

'Who is addressing me? The girl or the dragon?' roared the High Mermaid. 'Only one creature may stand on the Speaker's Rock. One of you must leave. Now!'

Hattie could feel a trembling Mith Ickle gently uncurl from her shoulders and flutter away.

'I am, Your Grace,' said Hattie, her voice

barely louder than a whisper, as Petunia had
advised.

'Speak up, girl,' said the High Mermaid.
'Tell me who you are!'

'I'm Hattie, Guardian of the creatures of the

magical Kingdom of Bellua, Your Grace,' replied Hattie, raising her voice a little, but not, she hoped, too much.

'Guardian of who?' shouted the High Mermaid. 'Are you trying to test my ears, girl? Stop mumbling at once!'

Resolving to raise her voice slightly again, Hattie remembered Petunia's second piece of advice: *Never repeat anything.*

'I have to help cure a poor mermaid who has lost her colours,' she said instead. 'Her name's Marina and –'

'I didn't ask you what you're doing or anything about a mermaid silly enough to lose something,' yelled the High Mermaid. 'I asked you of whom – or what – you are Guardian. Now answer me!'

Feeling a little confused, Hattie decided it was safest to just answer the question.

Satisfied, the High Mermaid carried on, 'So why do you think you can interrupt my busy day to help a careless mermaid?'

Anxious to leave the silver rock as quickly as possible, Hattie was tempted only to give the High Mermaid the facts: to explain about the threat of King Ivar, and Marina's predicament, and how only the rainbow syrup could help. But Petunia had been insistent that setting riddles was the key to pleasing the High Mermaid. Thinking of the kinds of rhymes

she had read in the big red book, Hattie came
up with the best she could on the spot:

A liquid that is bright and thick
Will help to cure a mermaid sick.
For just one cup is all I ask,
So that I might complete my task.

Hattie was congratulating herself on managing
not one rhyme but two when the piercing
voice of the High Mermaid rang in her ears.

'How dare you insult me with a silly riddle!
I asked you a simple question and you cannot
even offer a straightforward answer. Such
impertinence! I'll have you thrown out of my

Council. I'll have you banned from Bellua. I'll –'

Hattie immediately realized that Petunia's advice had been a trick. 'I'm very sorry, Your Grace,' she said, switching to a loud, clear voice. 'I didn't mean to insult you. I really didn't.'

'Then answer the question!' snapped the High Mermaid, fixing her steely eyes on Hattie's face. 'And make it quick.'

Hattie's heart sank. She was making such a mess of things!

Think on your feet and improvise, thought Hattie, remembering Uncle B's words at the village hall. *Convince the High Mermaid that she has to help me!*

'Marina has had her colours taken by Ivar, the evil Imp King who wants to use the powers he's stolen to take over Bellua. All I ask for is some syrup from the Rainbow Waterfall, to give Marina her colours back.' Hattie hoped the brief explanation would be enough, but the High Mermaid didn't seem convinced.

'Why should I give you, a young girl – although you say you're a Guardian – and your little dragon friend, anything?' she said.

'I have the star birthmark and the white streak of a Guardian,' said Hattie, indicating first her cheek and then her hair with a slightly shaky hand. 'And I really want to stop that puffed-up Ivar from hurting Bellua's magical creatures. It's the only way to protect the truly important ones, such as Your Grace. Ivar has to know he can't get away with this. He can't win!'

Instantly Hattie saw that her decision to flatter the High Mermaid had been the right one. Although the terrifying creature's voice was no friendlier, when she next addressed Hattie she did so a little less sternly.

'I may be able to spare you some syrup,' she said, 'if I could be sure you would be truly grateful.'

'Really I would,' replied Hattie. 'I know how precious it is to you, Your Grace, and that even being allowed here to ask for it is the greatest of honours. I'll use it wisely, I promise. I won't waste a drop.'

Hattie hoped she hadn't overdone the flattery, but the look on the High Mermaid's face told her she'd said the right thing.

'Take what you need,' said the High Mermaid. Then she gestured towards a red-haired mermaid near her. 'Direct this girl to the Rainbow Waterfall and allow her to fill one small shell. We cannot allow the Imp King to threaten our kind, and so the arrival of the Guardian is to be welcomed.'

Before Hattie could offer any thanks for either the syrup or the appreciation shown to her, the High Mermaid was in full flow again.

'Don't think it will be easy to scoop up the syrup, Guardian. It swirls in a fast-spinning whirlpool at the base of the Rainbow Waterfall, whizzed into dizzying circles by the force of it.'

Feeling a mixture of gratitude and fear, Hattie said goodbye and stepped off the silver rock, ready for her next challenge.

In a Whirl

Mith Ickle fluttered beside Hattie as they were directed to a rocky ledge at the top of the waterfall. They gazed at the torrent of liquid that thundered down in every colour of the rainbow.

'Wow!' said Hattie. 'That's *beautiful*!'

'And precious,' added a silver-haired mermaid who was perched on the ledge. 'If you want to

take a shellful of the syrup, you'll have to make your way down to the whirlpool. The rope ladder for land creatures is over there. You can use this to collect the syrup.'

Hattie took the empty shell that the mermaid

was holding out to her. She couldn't help but admire its smooth spiral shape and pale-cream sheen rippling like mother-of-pearl.

When she looked up, Hattie saw that the mermaid had already disappeared. The ladder she had mentioned hung from the far side of the ledge, reaching down to the bottom of the waterfall. It was made of thick, glossy olive-coloured seaweed and it swayed dangerously from side to side.

'I hope this'll take my weight,' said Hattie as she stepped on to the first rung. 'I'll meet you at the bottom, Mith.'

Seeing the splashes of syrup that hit Hattie as soon as she stepped down to the next rung,

Mith Ickle flew off immediately – she hated getting wet!

Hattie had to be very careful with her footing. Ignoring her nerves, she made steady progress, thinking of Marina all the time.

At the bottom of the ladder, Mith Ickle was pleased to see Hattie arrive safely, still clutching the shell.

Smiling with relief, Hattie turned to face the whirlpool. All the rainbow liquid of the waterfall met there in an amazing swirl, but the colours didn't merge into a muddy brown, like when Hattie mixed several different paints together. Instead they formed a multicoloured spiral, where red and blue whirled next to

purple, green, yellow, orange, turquoise and silver. The overall effect was so breathtaking that for a moment Hattie forgot why she was standing there.

'Take your syrup then.'

The voice made Hattie jump. To her left, several mermaids had lined up and were watching her.

Probably to keep a close eye on the precious liquid, Hattie thought.

'Scoop it up in your shell,' said a second mermaid.

'Yes, get on with it,' said a third.

Grumpy mermaids aside, Hattie knew that she ought to get a move on. Marina would be getting weaker by the minute and Hattie still had to find her way back to the Frozen Merlakes. She stepped towards the rocky edge of the whirlpool and peered in. The ledge she was standing on was a lot higher than the whirlpool, which meant she would have to lean over and reach down to fill up the shell. Hattie hoped her arms would be long enough.

She knelt down and stretched as far as she could. Although the shell brushed the surface of the syrup, none flowed inside. She tried again and again, but each time Hattie raised the still-empty shell she felt her frustration grow.

'There's got to be another way,' she huffed.

With Mith Ickle urging her to take care, she

again stretched as far as possible, gripping tightly to the edge of the rock. Above the sound of the fast-moving whirlpool, she could hear the mermaids laughing at her. Determined to prove them wrong and get back to Marina, Hattie made one final effort. Holding on to the rock, she stretched further down than before.

Suddenly she felt her hand slip, her body tip forward and her head hurtle towards the whirlpool! She heard Mith Ickle cry out and felt the dragon's claws uselessly scrabbling to grab her legs, but it was no good. Hattie took a deep breath and braced herself for the plunge into the pool. But, instead of getting wet, she

heard the rushing of air and felt herself being
pushed back on to the ledge.

The movement was so unexpected it took a
moment for Hattie to realize what had
happened. The mermaids had leapt into the

whirlpool to save her! Despite the force of the water, they floated effortlessly, swaying their tails gracefully to stay in the same place.

'Thank you so, so much!' cried Hattie. 'You saved me from falling in. I'm sure I'd have drowned without your help.'

The mermaids were in no mood to accept Hattie's words of gratitude, however.

'We can't have other creatures contaminating our whirlpool,' snapped one.

'Especially a human,' added another with a sneer.

'Even if she is a Guardian,' said a third.

Wondering if she would *ever* succeed in befriending a mermaid, Hattie glanced down, relieved to see the shell still in her hand. To her amazement, some syrup had been collected in it. She hoped it was enough to treat Marina, as she knew that asking for more would be out of the question.

'Come on, Mith,' she said. 'We've got that long windy path back to the merlakes. We'd better get going!'

However, before the two friends turned to go, one of the mermaids called out to her loudly. 'No, no, Hattie! You mustn't go the long way round. You *have* to go through the Ancient Desert or it'll be too late.'

Too late for what? wondered Hattie. Were the members of the Council concerned for their cousins at the merlakes after all?

A second mermaid confirmed her suspicions. 'You need to get that to Marina as soon as you can,' she said. 'Just the thought of her dull, lifeless tail makes me feel a bit queasy. Hurry!'

'But Marina's friends told me to avoid the Ancient Desert,' said Hattie, her head whirling in confusion. 'They said I'd get lost and my journey would take even longer.'

A loud snort exploded from the first mermaid, followed by an angry snarl. 'I hope you're not suggesting that the advice of lowly lake-dwellers is better than that of noble Council members, Guardian?'

Hattie looked at the mermaids' narrowed eyes and pursed lips and decided not to argue. 'No, of course not. The desert route it is then. I'm sure we'll find our way, won't we, Mith?'

The first mermaid's expression softened slightly. 'Stay on the path and look out for the sphinxes. Keep them on your right and you can't go wrong.'

Grateful for the advice, Hattie and Mith Ickle said their goodbyes and set off for the Ancient Desert.

Sounds in the Sand

The heat hit Hattie as soon as her feet sank into the warm desert sand. All around were golden dunes, the wide landscape dotted with the occasional rock or cactus. The still air warmed her throat and lungs and Hattie wished she'd brought a bottle of water with her. Not even the holiday the Bright family had

taken on a Greek island last summer had been this hot!

Determined not to lose her focus, Hattie squinted into the distance until she was sure she could see the sphinxes ahead. They were the landmark that told her she was heading the right way.

'If we stay on this path, we should be fine,' she said to Mith Ickle, striding forward. 'We'll be back at the merlakes in no time.'

At first, the two friends made good progress and the rainbow sky above the waterfall was soon far behind them. Every so often Hattie peered into the shell, checking that the precious multicoloured liquid was still there. Mith Ickle was flying so closely alongside her that the flap of her wings acted as a welcome cooling fan.

Suddenly a loud and familiar sound filled

the air around them. There was no mistaking the echoing cackle that whipped across the sand: King Ivar!

Worried, Hattie turned to Mith Ickle. 'Oh no! I might have guessed *he* wouldn't be far away! He must be after the rainbow syrup, Mith. We can't let him take it. It's our only chance to save Marina.'

Hattie spun round, trying to catch sight of the evil Imp King. But the laughter seemed to come from a different direction each time she heard it, and Ivar was nowhere to be seen.

'Can you see him from up there?' called Hattie as Mith Ickle flew high above the sandy landscape for a better view. But the little dragon shook her head. 'Well, we only have one choice,' said Hattie, 'and that's to keep going. Marina is counting on us.'

Hattie's heart pumped faster knowing that Ivar was following her through the desert. Every time his menacing cackle filled the air, her eyes darted left and right, trying to catch sight of him, though all she saw in the stark desert landscape were tiny ripples in the sand. She wasn't quite sure what the Imp King was planning to do, but she knew that she had to be prepared for anything.

'Ivar must have something else up his sleeve than that horrible laugh,' she said to Mith Ickle, trying to sound more relaxed than she felt. 'What do you think he'll do next?'

The answer came just moments later. Hattie jumped with surprise when Ivar suddenly appeared a few steps in front of her. His sharp features were fixed in a threatening grimace and his long cloak trailed behind him, whipping up sand as he continued his horrid cackling, closer than ever before.

'I'm not scared of you!' called Hattie bravely. 'You won't stop –'

Before Hattie could finish her sentence, she noticed that the desert sand had started to dance around her feet, forming itself into circular trails that threatened to envelop her.

'He's going to use Lunar's power to whip up a sandstorm!' cried Hattie. 'Quick, Mith – let's get out of the way!'

Hattie had only just jumped to one side when a bright flash of light shot across the desert, causing her to scrunch her eyes up tightly.

'You're not scared of me then, Hattie B?'

Another loud sinister laugh filled the air, fading as she peered through her fingers until a second flash came and then a third.

'You should be!' screeched Ivar loudly.

Hattie felt sharp pinpricks on her hands and face where grains of sand were swirling against her skin. Each time she dared to open her eyes, spots of light danced in front of them so she couldn't see where she was going.

Hattie found herself staggering across the sand blindly, her eyes watering and Mith Ickle puffing beside her. They could do nothing but stumble away from Ivar's threatening voice.

When at last the evil Imp King was silent and she could no longer feel the sand hitting her, Hattie carefully opened her eyes. Dismayed, she saw that they'd left the path and she had no idea in which direction she was going.

The bare desert had few landmarks, and every rock or cactus looked the same. With Ivar gone, the eerie silence was almost more scary than the echo of his maniacal laugh.

'Stay close!' Hattie called to Mith Ickle as she stumbled across the sand, eventually reaching a path that she hoped would take them out of the desert. 'If we can find the sphinxes, I reckon we'll be OK.'

'I can help,' replied Mith Ickle and she spread her wings as wide as she could and soared upward into the heat-glazed sky. 'Yes, I can see the sphinxes from here, Hattie,' she called. 'We're back on the right path. Carry on!'

Shaken by the appearance of Ivar and the confusing lights, Hattie found the walk harder than before. The hot desert air seemed even more stifling and her throat felt drier with every step. Worse still, she thought she could hear a faint cackle in the distance – and it seemed to be getting closer . . .

'What's that over there, Mith?' Hattie asked, spotting a strange ripple in the sand ahead of them. 'Are they . . . *ears*?'

The dragon nodded. There was no doubt about it — the tips of two pointy ears were poking out of a cluster of rocks and Hattie knew exactly who they belonged to.

'So Ivar's using Marina's power of camouflage to hide in the rocks! Except he doesn't seem to have mastered hiding his whole body — at least not yet . . .' Hattie said nervously.

Hattie watched as Ivar's ears were quickly joined by his sharp-featured face, then his cloaked shoulders and finally his spindly legs as he appeared from the rocks in front of her.

She was still looking on in amazement when

Mith Ickle cried, 'Watch out, Hattie! He's
going to grab the syrup!'

'I'll have that!' Ivar said gleefully. An evil
grin spread across his face as he leapt up and
shot out a skinny arm towards Hattie.

'Oh no you don't!' yelled Hattie, jumping to one side and leaving Ivar clutching at thin air.

In seconds, Ivar had disappeared back into his sandy camouflage so Hattie crouched down, preparing for his next ambush.

She felt a rush of air as Ivar appeared beside her, flapping his tiny wings, his cloak billowing around him.

'Give me the rainbow syrup, Guardian!' he screeched, grabbing Hattie's hands. 'NOW!'

Hattie pulled her hands free, still holding the shell, and tried to run, but the Imp King flew round her, blocking her way. When she ducked low to escape him, she saw the sand begin to move in threatening swirls again until it stabbed

at her cheeks and got in her eyes. Without thinking, she lifted her hand to shield her face.

Ivar took his chance. He swooped and snatched the shell!

'Give it back!' yelled Hattie, lunging towards the sneering imp and grabbing at his cloak as it trailed behind him.

'Too late!' he cackled. 'You'll never catch me now. A weak human like you never had a chance against me, Hattie B! I'm the mighty King Ivar. Next time we meet, you'll be bowing down to me, the all-powerful ruler of Bellua!'

With that, he jumped into the air, frantically flapping his little imp wings until he rose above the desert floor.

With a gasp of horror, Mith Ickle soared up to follow him, but Hattie urged her back. 'It's too dangerous, Mith. Leave him – I don't want you to get us into more trouble than we're already in.'

Hattie put her head in her hands in despair. With no way to cure Marina, she really had no idea what to do next. *If things don't go to plan, you'll have to think on your feet*, Uncle B had said.

'Think, Hattie, think!' she scolded herself, cross that she'd lost the rainbow syrup.

Mith Ickle flew down to comfort her. 'I'm sorry. I should have seen that coming,' she said, peering up from beneath her long eyelashes. 'I wish I could help.'

Suddenly Hattie had an idea. 'It's OK, Mith. I think I know what to do,' she said, her face brightening. 'Did you say we're still on the right path?'

The little dragon flew up quickly to check, nodding enthusiastically to confirm that they were.

'Maybe what we need is a creature that's bigger and stronger than either of us — or Ivar. Come on, Mith — let's hurry to the sphinxes. I think they could be the answer.'

Taken for a Ride

The two sphinxes loomed high above them. Hattie was amazed at their enormous size.

'Don't be offended if they're not very responsive. They don't usually talk much,' Mith Ickle warned Hattie.

Hattie felt a flicker of doubt creep in.

They're so still and quiet, she thought. *Perhaps they won't be any use to us at all.*

Their heads were considerably higher than hers, so Hattie spoke as loudly as she could. 'Hello, I'm Hattie, Guardian of the creatures here in Bellua. I hope you don't mind, but I wondered if I could ask for some help?' Receiving no response, as Mith Ickle had predicted, Hattie pressed on anyway. 'A mermaid called Marina desperately needs my help and Ivar, the evil Imp King, has stolen the magic syrup I need to cure her.'

The two sphinxes slowly dipped their heads towards Hattie and she felt a flash of hope. Then one of them spoke in a voice so soft that Hattie had to cup one ear to hear her.

The words made her stomach do a sudden

flip. Had the sphinx really said what Hattie thought she'd said? Were the sphinxes on Ivar's side after all?

'I'm sorry. I'm not sure I heard you properly,' shouted Hattie, even louder, determined not to be misheard herself. 'Did you say, "Ivar's right"?'

The second sphinx lowered her head and Hattie moved as close as she could to hear the whispered answer. When the second sphinx had spoken, she gasped. It seemed she had stumbled across two of Ivar's supporters!

'Perhaps we should go, Mith,' said Hattie, trying to keep her voice calm. 'I think the first sphinx said she could see that Ivar was right, and now the second has just told me that they trust him! I don't think we're going to find any help here. Let's go!'

Mith Ickle turned to Hattie, a questioning look on her face. 'Are you sure you aren't being a bit hasty?' she asked. 'One of my dragon friends passed over the Ancient Desert a few days ago. He told me that he and the sphinxes had talked about how terrible things would be if Ivar took control of Bellua.'

For a moment Hattie wasn't sure what to do. As she wiped the sweat from her forehead, Uncle B's words swam around her head: *Think on your feet, think on your feet . . .*

'You're right, Mith,' she said, turning back

to the enormous creatures. 'I can't have heard right. I have to get closer!'

Mith Ickle watched with surprise as Hattie began to clamber clumsily up one of the sphinx's legs and on to her back.

The sphinx didn't object to her being there, so Hattie felt brave enough to question the giant creature again. 'Do you think you might be able to help me find Ivar? I'm pretty sure he's still in the desert somewhere but he's not easy to spot. You're so tall – I'm sure I could find him in no time from up here.'

The sphinx slowly turned her head towards Hattie's. Up close, there was no mistaking the sphinx's reply. 'Of course we'll help you,

Guardian. We saw Ivar's light,' whispered the sphinx. 'We must stop him!'

Hattie couldn't believe she had misheard the two gentle creatures! How could she have mistaken *light* for *right*, and *must* for *trust*?

'Thank you so much!' Hattie said with relief.

The sphinx stiffly raised her heavy back legs, lifting Hattie high off the ground, while Mith Ickle flapped joyfully beside her. Hattie had a much better view now, but she still couldn't see Ivar.

All of a sudden the sphinx began to move forward slowly, placing one large stone paw down in front of the other.

Hattie gasped with delight.

'I didn't know you could walk!' she exclaimed.

As the sphinx stretched her legs out, she gradually began to speed up. Hattie's hair streamed behind her and Mith Ickle snorted happy puffs of smoke as they made their way across the desert in search of Ivar.

'We mustn't stop until we find him,' Hattie urged her new friend.

She listened out for Ivar's tell-tale cackle, but the only sound she could hear was the tread of the sphinx's heavy feet on the sand and the flap of Mith Ickle's wings beside her. She was just beginning to lose hope again when she craned her head a little higher and spotted something in the distance that made her yelp with delight.

Perched behind a silvery rock was a small creature with very pointy ears – he was facing away from them and a shimmering shell was grasped in his long, gnarled fingers . . .

'He's there! Ivar's over there!' Hattie cried. 'I'm sorry to ask when you've been so helpful already,' she continued, leaning towards the sphinx's right ear, 'but is there any chance you could go even a tiny bit faster? The quicker I get that syrup back, the better!'

The sphinx understood the urgency and picked up her pace in seconds. Hattie found herself being thrown from side to side so held on tightly. At one point, she felt herself slide so far to one side she thought she might fall off the creature completely, but, with some careful wriggling, she managed to pull herself back up.

'Hold tight, Hattie!' called Mith Ickle, who was flying alongside as fast as she could, puffing as the desert heat began to affect even her.

'I will!' replied Hattie, wishing she'd joined Chloe for her horse-riding lessons.

Hattie, Mith and the sphinx slowed to a quiet crawl as they got nearer. Ivar was so engrossed in admiring his stolen booty that he didn't notice their arrival until they were quite close.

When he saw them at last, a look of horror

and disbelief crossed his sharp features, and
Ivar began frantically flapping his tiny wings,
the shell of syrup in his hand. The panicked
imp fluttered upward, keeping his gaze fixed
firmly on the sphinx, who was getting ready

to pounce. He didn't notice the huge cactus behind him until it was too late!

Hattie watched in amusement as Ivar flew straight into the cactus's sharp spikes, which caught the fabric of his cloak and pinned him firmly to the top of the plant's fleshy stalk. No amount of writhing could set him free.

'Looks like you're in a *prickle*, Ivar!' she teased as the sphinx calmly brought her to the Imp King's side. 'And I'll have my shell back too, thanks.'

Hattie reached towards him, but Ivar was quicker. He swiftly hid the shell under his cloak and Hattie yelped with pain as her hand brushed the cactus's sharp spikes.

'I can help,' said Mith Ickle, flying towards Ivar and using her snout to lift his heavy cloak.

Once the shell was revealed, Hattie reached for it again, this time successfully releasing it from Ivar's grip.

'Bye, Ivar!' called Hattie as the sphinx turned towards the path that would take her back to the Frozen Merlakes. 'Better luck next time, eh?'

Ivar didn't answer her, but Hattie knew that the image of him dangling by his cloak from the cactus plant would keep her amused for a long time.

'Immie! Immie! Help me!' Ivar called.

'IMMIE! Where are you? Come and help me! NOW!'

Then, with a final *harrumph*, he fired a flash of light, which shot straight to the ground, dazzling nothing more than a small rock.

Riding on the sphinx, it didn't take long for Hattie to reach the edge of the desert. She carefully slid herself down the shoulder of the graceful creature and checked that the syrup was still safely inside the shell.

'I can't tell you how grateful I am,' she said. 'You've saved me and the mermaid

Marina — and possibly all the creatures of Bellua! Thank you!'

As she said her goodbyes, Hattie thought the sphinx whispered, '*You're welcome,*' in reply, although she couldn't be sure. Then the giant creature was gone, and Hattie knew the next stage of her adventure was about to begin.

'Right, Mith, back to the merlakes we go. Let's hope that this rainbow syrup does the trick and gives Marina back her colours!'

A Special Souvenir

The coolness of the merlakes was a welcome change after the stifling heat of the desert. As soon as they reached the edge of the first icy pool, Hattie scooped up a handful of the clear water and drank it gratefully. Now she felt ready to cure her patient.

Hattie and Mith Ickle found Marina again easily as she was now surrounded by an even larger group than before. Some were fanning her with large pieces of pondweed and others were moistening her dry lips with small chunks of ice they had prised off the rocks nearby.

'I'm back,' said Hattie, ignoring one mermaid who muttered, '*About time!*' under her breath. 'I've got the rainbow syrup here.'

Marina was too weak even to look up. Her hair was even more dull and untidy than before and her eyes were half-closed.

Her companions seemed concerned and one addressed Hattie in the friendliest voice she had ever heard a mermaid use: 'We know Marina's young, but she will be OK, won't she?'

'I hope so,' replied Hattie. 'Let's not waste any more time before we find out.'

Cupping Marina's drooping head in one hand, Hattie held the shell over the mermaid's pale lips and began to slowly drip the thick syrup on to them. The first two or three drops had little effect, but by the fourth or fifth Hattie was certain she could see a tinge of pink at the end of Marina's tail. Nine or ten drops in, the pink had spread further up her tail, joined by some blue, green and yellow.

When half the syrup had been used, not only were waves of colour spreading almost all the way up Marina's tail but her hair seemed to have brightened and small rose-coloured blushes had appeared on her cheeks.

With new-found strength, Marina swallowed a large glug. The effect was instant! A rainbow swept up and down her tail, the colours mingling in a kaleidoscope of patterns. For the first time since Hattie had met her, Marina raised her head fully and looked longingly towards the lake.

'Time for a swim?' asked Hattie, watching as Marina slid gracefully into the cool water and vanished into its depths. The mermaids who had been with her followed.

'Thank you, Hattie,' they called as they drifted away.

Marina reappeared at the lake's edge moments later. 'I can't thank you enough, Hattie,' she said, raising her now-cheerful and bright-eyed face out of the water, which shimmered with all the hues in her healed tail.

Clasped in one hand was a beautiful orange shell with a silvery spiral pattern running round it.

'Hold out your hand,' said Marina, and as Hattie did so the mermaid tipped the contents of the shell on to it.

At first, all Hattie could see was a dazzling cloud of colours swirling around her open palm. However, as they spiralled away into the icy air, Hattie spotted a small mermaid charm.

'Thank you, Marina. It's beautiful!' Hattie said, attaching it to her bracelet straight away.

The mermaid smiled, then, leaving a

multicoloured ripple that disappeared into the lake, she left Hattie and went to catch up with her friends.

'Well, Ivar may have her powers, but he hasn't succeeded in hurting her like he wanted to. Let's head back,' Hattie said, smiling as Mith Ickle settled into her usual place round the Guardian's shoulders.

She picked up the shell with the few remaining drops of rainbow syrup, and they set off for the cave.

With no sign of Ivar, Hattie and Mith Ickle skirted the Enchanted Orchard and were making their way to Dragon's Valley when they spotted a small creature with distinctive

blue hair, stomping towards Pixie Park. She
was scattering items of clothing as she went,
muttering angrily about 'a silly useless disguise'
before declaring that she wouldn't help 'that
bossy Ivar' again.

'So it *was* Immie pretending to be Petunia

after all!' cried Hattie. 'I'm so sorry I didn't listen to you, Mith. She had me completely fooled.'

'Never mind,' said Mith Ickle kindly. 'Sometimes it's hard to guess someone's true intentions. I'm sure you wouldn't have believed a dragon would want to be friends with a human when we first met either.'

'You're right,' laughed Hattie. 'But I'm glad I was proved wrong. You're one of the best friends I've got.'

Hattie hoped that saying this wasn't being disloyal to Chloe. But the real world and Bellua seemed so far apart, so she thought it was probably OK to have a best friend in each. She

did wish that Chloe could join her on her
magical adventures, though.

To Hattie's relief, they arrived at the cave door
without running into any further trouble. She
had been half-expecting to hear Ivar's cackle
again but the only sounds had been the friendly
greetings of passing unicorns, dragons and the
occasional fairy.

'He must still be stuck on that cactus!' she
said, laughing.

Inside the cave it was even quieter. Hattie
reached for an empty potion bottle from one
of the heavily laden shelves and carefully

poured the last drops of rainbow syrup into it.

Once she had labelled it neatly, she returned the bottle to the shelf, where it sat among the many ingredients collected by generations of

Guardians before her – and the three she had filled on her previous adventures. Both she and Mith Ickle knew that this ritual meant that another visit was coming to an end, and the little dragon used her pink snout to push Hattie's vet's bag across the stone table towards her.

'Take the shell with you as a souvenir,' Mith Ickle said, but Hattie looked doubtful. Would it be safe to take items from Bellua into the real world? Would it give her away and cause her to break her secret oath?

'You could hide it in your bag?' suggested Mith Ickle, sensing Hattie's unease.

'Good idea,' agreed Hattie, dropping the

beautiful iridescent shell into the now-shimmering bag. 'Bye, Mith. I'm sure I'll see you again soon. Ivar's stolen another power and I don't suppose it'll be long before he decides to add another to his collection. Maybe next time I can stop him – for good!'

Mith Ickle's melodic farewell rang out as Hattie peered into the vet's bag and the familiar tumbling sensation transported her away from Bellua and back to the real world, where she knew Chloe was anxiously waiting for her.

Picture Perfect

Hattie watched the sparkly vet's bag slowly turn back to dull leather. She peered inside to check that the shell was still there, and she couldn't resist taking it out quickly to admire its stunning colours. As Hattie held it up to the light, she gasped. Its amazing beauty stood out even more against the backdrop of her boring, normal bedroom. With a sigh, she placed the shell back inside the bag, knelt on the floor and pushed it deep underneath her bed.

Remembering the reason she'd given Chloe for leaving the village hall, Hattie looked quickly around her room for something to take back with her as a prop. Seeing a beaded bracelet on her bedside table, she slid it on to her wrist above the charm bracelet with its newly attached mermaid.

I'll tell Chloe it's my lucky acting charm, thought Hattie. *She did catch me looking at my wrist after all, so she might be convinced.*

Preparing to race back to the village hall,

Hattie galloped down the stairs and hurtled through the front door.

Hattie slipped into the village hall just in time to hear a loud announcement boom through the speakers: 'PLEASE PUT YOUR HANDS TOGETHER TO WELCOME THE CAST OF THE JUNIOR DRAMA PRESENTATION TO THE STAGE.'

A wave of applause filled the hall as Hattie joined the line of children waiting backstage. She was still a little out of breath and hadn't had time to check her appearance, but at least she wasn't late.

From her position at the front of the line, Chloe turned back and smiled quizzically at her friend. Hattie smiled back, raising her wrist and pointing at the beaded bracelet. She mouthed something about it being lucky and wondered whether Chloe would understand what she was saying better than she had understood the sphinxes in Bellua!

The play was over in a flash. Hattie had managed to remember all her lines and felt elated when the cast took their bows as the audience clapped enthusiastically. She could see her parents a few rows from the front, with a beaming Uncle B cheering beside them. Even her brother, Peter, was slouched against the back wall of the hall, clapping loudly. Once the applause had died down, the cast filed off the stage and Hattie found herself beside Chloe again.

'Did you say Victoria did your hair?' asked Chloe, gently guiding Hattie towards the large mirror backstage.

Hattie looked into the silvery glass. 'I knew I shouldn't have trusted her!' she said, seeing that Victoria had tied her hair into two bunches that were at such different heights they looked completely ridiculous. 'Oh well, it didn't seem

to stop the audience from enjoying the play, I suppose.'

'D'you like your hair then, Hattie?' sneered Victoria as she walked past with Louisa and Jodie, who were smirking on either side of her.

'It's nice and quirky,' replied Hattie, determined not to show Victoria that she cared.

Realizing that she wasn't going to provoke an argument, Victoria moved on, muttering under her breath that '*quirky* was *one* word for hair like that'. Though Hattie heard her mean classmate perfectly, she just laughed as she tugged both bunches free and swept her hair up into her signature ponytail.

'That's better,' said Chloe. 'You look like you again. Now, aren't there loads of stalls outside that we can have a go on?'

Once the two girls had tried their luck at the teddy tombola, bought a cupcake each — and even had a go on Peter's penalty shoot-out stall, they found themselves by a sign saying FUNNY PHOTOS.

They were deciding whether to spend their last bit of money there when the stallholder appeared by Hattie's side.

'Aha! Some new customers! You take your places and I'll take a . . . um . . . a photo. Yes, a photo. That's what this stall is all about.'

'Uncle B!' said Hattie. 'I didn't know you were running a stall!'

Uncle B indicated a giant wooden hoarding behind him and Hattie could hardly believe what she was seeing. Painted in vivid glowing colours was a beautiful underwater scene, where a couple of mermaids posed elegantly among bright fishes. The only thing missing from the magical scene were the faces of two mermaids, which had been cut out from the wood.

'Why don't you two best friends poke your heads through those holes? Then I'll take a photo and you can pretend you're two beautiful mermaids who live in an amazing magical land,' said Uncle B.

'Ooh yes, let's!' said Chloe eagerly. 'Come on, Hattie! You can be the dark-haired mermaid and I'll be the blonde one.'

With their heads poking through to complete the picture, both girls looked directly into Uncle B's camera.

'Give me nice big mermaid smiles!' he called – and Hattie was sure that Uncle B gave her a little wink as the camera clicked.

Hattie looked at Chloe smiling next to her. Would she ever be able to take her best friend to Bellua to meet Mith Ickle and all her other magical friends? Hattie wasn't sure, but, thinking of the five charms that hung from her bracelet, she guessed it wouldn't be long before she added a sixth.

Next time, she would find a way to stop King Ivar. Even if Hattie could cure them, he

had to stop hurting the creatures. She knew Ivar wouldn't give up without a fight — and she hoped that, with or without Chloe, she would be strong enough for the battle ahead.

If you can't wait for
the next adventure of

here is an exclusive preview of

The Pony's Hoof

Telling Tales

Hattie threw open the wooden door at the back of the cave. A huge crowd of animals had gathered outside and there was a collected cheer as they spotted the Guardian.

She waved in surprise as she took in the amazing scene. Creatures of all shapes, sizes and shades mingled together in a sea of colours. While some animals stood on the soft velvety grass, above them fairies and sprites flitted, their shimmering wings creating sparks in Bellua's bright sky. Tiny pixies and imps peeped out between the legs of unicorns and trolls, and even the sphinxes were there.

Hattie couldn't begin to count how many had come to greet her. Nor could she work out what any of them were saying!

The high voices of the smaller creatures merged with the low voices of the larger ones, getting louder and louder . . .

Then suddenly the much deeper sound of an animal clearing his throat filled the air and everyone went quiet. When he stepped forward, Hattie recognized him immediately: it was Themis, leader of the unicorns.

'My friends,' began Themis, addressing the crowd. 'Let's not all speak together. We must welcome our Guardian. She is here to help us defeat Ivar, the evil Imp King, whose wickedness is spreading further into our beautiful land.'

Themis turned his majestic head to Hattie. 'What the creatures tell you is true. Ivar has attempted to steal more of our precious magical powers. We cannot be more thankful that you are here again to aid us in our struggle and we want you to know that we will be there if you need our help.'

There was a murmur of agreement from the gathering and Hattie bowed her head in gratitude.

'I'll do all I can to help you defeat Ivar,' she said. Scanning the magical creatures before her, she asked, 'Someone must need my help now – who has met Ivar today?'

There was movement in the crowd and Hattie saw a small horse-like creature with silky ebony-black hair hobble slowly towards the front. At first she thought it was another unicorn, but then she noticed the wings folded by his side. It was a baby pegasus!

Hattie immediately made her way to the young pegasus and knelt down to examine him. The murmur of noise from the crowd began to build, and Hattie couldn't hear what he was saying.

She stood up and addressed the crowd again. 'Thank you so much for coming here, and for trusting me to help you. I will do my very best,' she promised. 'I have to take this little one to my cave for treatment but I really hope to meet you all again soon.'

Themis started off a chorus of goodbyes that sailed through Bellua's lightly shimmering sky as Hattie led the limping pegasus away.

Mith Ickle closed the wooden door and Hattie reached for the big red book, *Healing Magickal Beastes & Creatures*, which many generations of Guardians had used to find cures.

She turned to her patient. He looked up at her, his large chocolate-brown eyes full of sadness. 'I know Ivar had something to do with this,' she began, 'but can you tell me exactly what happened? Then I'm sure I'll be able to help you.'

When Hattie saw a tear roll down the young creature's face, she put her fingers between his soft ears and gave him a soothing stroke.

The pegasus nuzzled against her and Hattie could feel his small body trembling before he had even spoken a word. Just what had Ivar done to terrify him and leave him barely able to walk?

Hattie listened carefully as he began his story.

Will Hattie B succeed in helping the magical
creatures in the Kingdom of Bellua to overcome
King Ivar's wicked plans?

Don't miss

The Pony's Hoof

and

The Phoenix's Flame

Hattie will face her enemy once and for all,
with a little help from some
very loyal friends . . .

www.worldofhattieb.com

Homemade
Rainbow Syrup
for two

What you'll need:

- A selection of fruit juices e.g. orange, apple, cranberry (about 500ml in total)
- Ice-cube trays
- Lemonade
- Two glasses

What to do:

Carefully pour the fruit juices into the ice-cube trays and then pop them in the freezer for 2–3 hours.

Once the juice is frozen, push the cubes from the tray and put them in your glasses – try to use a mixture of different flavours and colours – and then top up with lemonade. Delicious!

Word Search

Can you help Hattie find the five missing words from the word search?

Bellua
Hattie
Immie
Mith
Vet

N	T	S	I	W	A	D	C	T	W
R	T	G	M	R	L	M	I	T	H
B	B	N	M	W	B	H	X	B	H
E	B	E	I	T	S	P	E	U	V
L	V	K	E	U	I	O	Q	L	R
L	L	Y	J	G	T	H	A	N	L
U	J	Y	F	H	U	V	T	D	U
A	H	A	T	T	I	E	A	Q	A
Z	P	A	Z	W	P	T	O	G	P
A	S	G	I	O	O	K	F	G	O

Visit **www.worldofhattieb.com** to check your answers.

Hattie B
Magical Vet

Find out more about
Hattie B
and the creatures
from the
Kingdom of
Bellua
by visiting

www.worldofhattieb.com